Written by **EVE BUNTING**

Illustrated by **DAVID DIAZ**

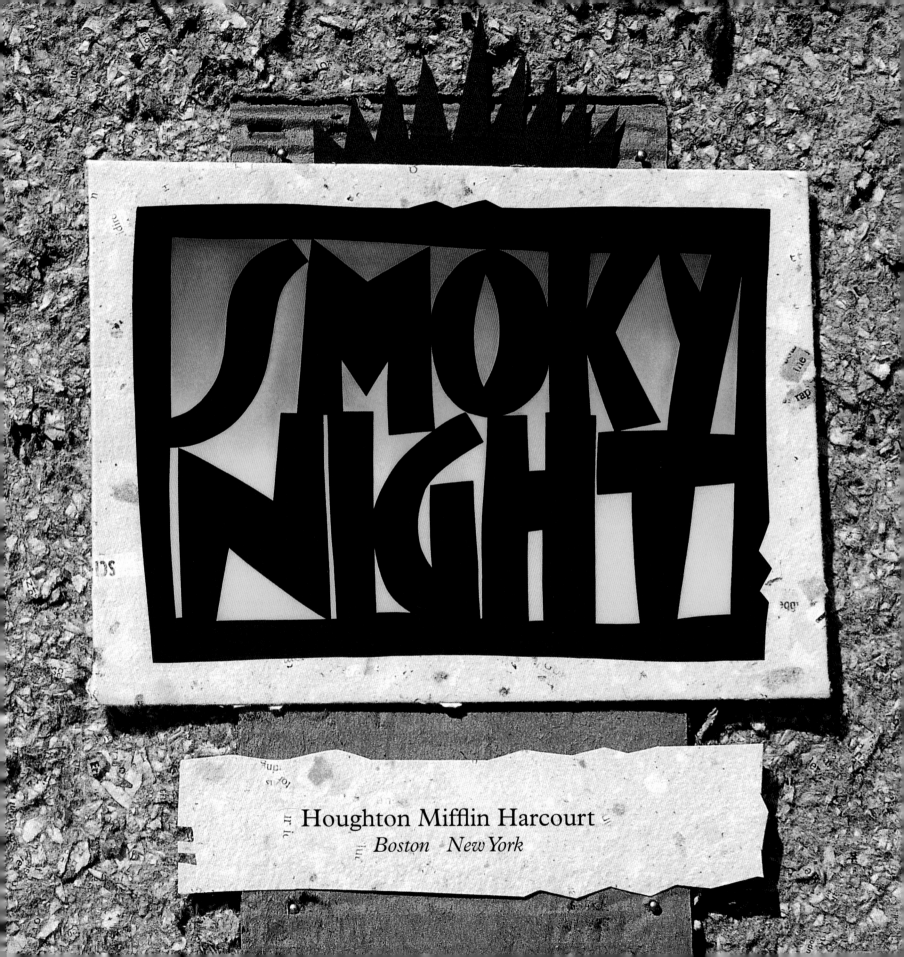

SMOKY NIGHT

Houghton Mifflin Harcourt
Boston New York

For information about permission to reproduce selections from this book, write
to trade.permissions@hmhco.com or to Permissions, Houghton Mifflin Harcourt
Publishing Company, 3 Park Avenue, 19th Floor, New York, New York 10016.

www.hmhco.com

Library of Congress Cataloging-in-Publication Data
Bunting, Eve, 1928–
Smoky night /by Eve Bunting ; illustrated by David Diaz.
p.   cm.
Summary: When the Los Angeles riots break out in the streets of their
neighborhood, a young boy and his mother learn the value of getting
along with others, no matter what their background or nationality.
ISBN-13: 978-0-15-269954-3   ISBN-10: 0-15-269954-6
ISBN-13: 978-0-15-201884-9 pb   ISBN-10: 0-15-201884-0 pb
1. Riots—California—Los Angeles—Juvenile fiction. [1. Riots—
California—Los Angeles—Fiction.   2. Interpersonal relations—
Fiction.   3. Neighborliness—Fiction.]   1. Diaz, David, ill.
II. Title.
PZ7.B9152751   1994
[E]—dc20   93-14885

SCP   39 38 37 36 35
4500794521

Printed in China

For the peacekeepers
—E. B.

For Gabrielle, my little Sweet Pea
—D. D.

Mama and I stand well back from our window, looking down. I'm holding Jasmine, my cat. We don't have our lights on though it's almost dark.

People are rioting in the street below.

Mama explains about rioting. "It can happen when people get angry. They want to smash and destroy. They don't care anymore what's right and what's wrong."

Below us they are smashing everything. Windows, cars, streetlights.

"They look angry. But they look happy, too," I whisper.

"After a while it's like a game," Mama says.

Two boys are carrying a TV from Morton's Appliances. It's hard for them because the TV is so heavy.

"Are they stealing it?" I ask.

Mama nods.

Someone breaks the window of Fashion Shoes. Two women and a man climb in through the broken glass. They toss out shoes like they're throwing footballs. I've never heard anybody laugh the way they laugh.

Smoke drifts, light as fog. I see the distant flicker of flames.

Across the street from us people are dragging cartons of cereal and sacks of rice from Kim's Market.

My mama and I don't go in Mrs. Kim's market even though it's close. Mama says it's better if we buy from our own people.

Mrs. Kim's cat and my cat fight all the time, and Mrs. Kim yells at Jasmine in words I can't understand. She's yelling the same kind of words now at the people who are stealing her stuff.

They pay no attention.

I move behind Mama. "Will they come here?"

"There's nothing for them here, Daniel. See? They've finished with our street. They're moving on."

Our street is emptying. One last man is staggering under a pile of clothes he's taken from the dry cleaners. The plastic bags are still over them.

"We'll sleep together tonight," Mama tells me.

She makes me wash my face and brush my teeth. I'm to take off my shoes but leave on my clothes.

She puts me next to the wall. I hold Jasmine.

"I can't sleep," I say.

"Shh!" Mama whispers. "Close your eyes."

I do.

I guess I sleep.

Next thing I know, Mama is shaking me.

"Quick, Daniel! Get up!"

There's a terrible smell of smoke. Someone's pounding on our apartment door. "Fire! Fire!"

I'm suddenly awake. "Where's Jasmine?" I run to the closet. Sometimes Jasmine sleeps on a shelf.

Mama's screaming at me. "We can't wait. Jasmine's gone. Put on your shoes. Hurry!"

We rush down the stairs. Others crowd around us. The smoke makes me cough.

Mr. Ramirez is in front of us carrying Lissa and the baby, who are both howling.

"Those people are hooligans," he shouts over his shoulder. "Hooligans!"

Mrs. Ramirez is ahead of him. She's holding the cage with Loco, their parrot. Loco's squawking something awful.

"Did you see Jasmine, Mr. Ramirez?" I shout.

He shakes his head, but I don't think he even hears me. "Don't touch the railing," he warns. "It's hot."

Outside, the sky is hazy orange. Flames pounce up the side of our building.

Three fire engines scream to a stop. Fire fighters jump out, running, pulling hoses. I see our window where Mama and I had stood. The fire hasn't reached it yet.

"Is everybody out?" one fire fighter yells.

"Far as we know," another says.

"Did you see a cat?" I ask him. "She's yellow. Maybe she's still in there."

He glances down. "Probably not, son. Cats are plenty smart. She'll be long gone."

A lady comes up to us. "There's a shelter you can come to," she says. "Everyone follow me."

I'm crying because I'm not sure Jasmine is all that smart. What if she's still inside?

Some of the streetlights have been smashed. We walk along the sidewalk, which sparkles with broken glass. There are empty cartons everywhere. A street sign lies crumpled in the gutter. I grab hold of Mama because I think I see a dead man with no arms lying there, too. But it's just one of those plastic people that show off clothes in department stores.

The lady looks back at Mrs. Kim, who is trailing along behind us. "Are you all right?" she calls.

Mrs. Kim nods.

"We're almost at the shelter," the lady tells her.

The shelter is in a church hall. There are cots to sleep on and a table with hot drinks. Two men are making sandwiches. I've never seen a bigger jar of mayo.

We see people from our building. They're talking about who did this. What will happen to us?

"It's a sad, sad night," Mr. Jackson says.

I ask him about Jasmine.

He says he's pretty sure he saw her. "She got out, Daniel," he tells me. I hope he's not just trying to make me feel better.

"Did you see *my* cat?" Mrs. Kim asks. "He is orange."

"He's the color of carrots," I say, and I almost add, "and he's fat and mean." But I don't.

A girl gives me a mug of hot chocolate. I wish it had more sugar. When I finish drinking it Mama says I should lie down. She's always making me lie down.

People keep coming. Some of them are crying. One woman screams and screams. I hide under my blanket.

Then Mama says, "Daniel! Look!"

And there is the fire fighter who was at our building. He is standing in the open door, with the smoky night behind him, and I see that he's carrying a cat under each arm. That was how Mr. Ramirez carried Lissa and the baby. The cats are howling, too.

"Jasmine!" The blanket's caught on my foot and I'm trailing it. "Oh, thank you! Thank you for finding her!"

"The other cat is mine." Mrs. Kim takes her big, fat, mean old orange cat and holds him close. I'm kissing Jasmine. She smells of smoke.

"Where was she?" I ask the fire fighter.

"The two of them were under the stairs, yowling and screeching," he says. He takes a mug of hot chocolate. I like him so much! I wish I had a whole barrel of sugar for his drink.

"The cats were together?" Mrs. Kim asks.

The fire fighter nods. "They were so scared they were holding paws."

I grin. "No, they weren't!"

"What about our building?" Mr. Ramirez asks.

"The fire's out. You'll be able to go back in a day or two."

A woman puts down a dish of milk. "Here kitty, kitty," she calls.

Jasmine jumps out of my arms, and Mrs. Kim puts her carrot-colored cat down, too. The cats drink from the same dish. Milk isn't that good for cats, but I don't say that either.

"Look at that!" Mama is all amazed. "I thought those two didn't like each other."

"They probably didn't know each other before," I explain. "Now they do."

Everyone looks at me, and it's suddenly very quiet.

"Did I say something wrong?" I whisper to Mama.

"No, Daniel." Mama's tugging at her fingers the way she does when she's nervous. "My name is Gena," she tells Mrs. Kim. "Perhaps when things settle down you and your cat will come over and share a dish of milk with us."

I think that's pretty funny, but nobody laughs.

Mrs. Kim picks up her cat and strokes him. She's staring at the wall. Maybe she's not going to say anything.

But then she looks across at Mama. "Thank you," she says. "We will come."

Mama smiles.

I reach out and stroke Mrs. Kim's big old orange cat, too. "Can you hear him, Mrs. Kim?" I ask. "He's purring!"

The paintings in this book were done in acrylics
on Arches watercolor paper. The backgrounds were
composed and photographed by the illustrator.
The title type was hand-lettered by the illustrator.
The display type was set in Kabel Ultra by Central Graphics,
San Diego, California.
The text type was set in Syntax Bold by Thompson Type,
San Diego, California.
Color separations by Bright Arts Ltd., Singapore
Printed and bound by RR Donnelley, China
Production supervision by Warren Wallerstein and Kent MacElwee
Designed by David Diaz and Lydia D'moch